IF I WERE QUEEN OF THE WORLD

Other books illustrated by Mark Graham:

Charlie Anderson
Home by Five
Michael and the Cats
Roommates
Roommates Again
Roommates and Rachel

Margaret K. McElderry Books

If I Were Queen of the World

of the World

WRITTEN BY FRED HIATT

ILLUSTRATED BY MARK GRAHAM

Margaret K. McElderry Books

To Deborah and Alexandra, two wonderful older sisters,
and Joseph, a terrific younger brother, with love.
—F. H.

To Margaret
—M. G.

MARGARET K. McELDERRY BOOKS
25 YEARS • 1972–1997

Margaret K. McElderry Books
An imprint of Simon & Schuster Children's Publishing Division
1230 Avenue of the Americas
New York, NY 10020

Book design by Angela Carlino
The text of this book was set in Modern MT
The illustrations were rendered in oil paint

Printed in the United States of America
First edition
10 9 8 7 6 5 4 3 2 1
Library of Congress Cataloging-in-Publication Data
Hiatt, Fred.
If I were queen of the world / Fred Hiatt ;
illustrated by Mark Graham—1st ed.
p. cm.
Summary: A young girl imagines all the wonderful things
she could have and do if she were queen of the world and her
little brother were her mere subject.
ISBN 0-689-80700-7
[Imagination—Fiction. 2. Brothers and sisters—Fiction.]
I. Graham, Mark, 1952- ill. II. Title.
PZ7.H495If 1997
[E]—dc20
95-45468
CIP   AC

If I were queen of the whole wide world, I'd have one hundred lollipops a day and never have to share.

But sometimes I'd let my little brother have a lick or two.

If I were queen of the whole wide world, I'd stay up as late as I wanted every night.

But I'd keep my brother company at bedtime,
just so he wouldn't be too lonely.

If I were queen of the world, I'd play hopscotch until my feet wore out, and it would always be my turn.

But once in a while I wouldn't get mad if my
brother messed up the chalk.

If I were queen of the world, I'd have my very own desk, which nobody else could ever touch.

But now and then, I might let my brother work with me.

If I were queen of the world, I'd have my very own
dog, too, who would come only when I called.

But my brother could pat her if he liked.

If I were queen of all the world, I'd ride the scariest roller coaster at the fair one hundred times in a row.

But if he wanted, I'd get off to keep my brother company on the flying baby elephants.

If I were queen of the world, I'd own so many
rubies and diamonds and emeralds that I could
swim in them.

But I'd turn a few of them into marbles for my little brother to play with.

If I were queen of the world, I'd have magic
powers and would fly above my fields and
woods and castles just by spreading my arms.

Sometimes I'd take my brother on my back.

If I were queen of the world, I'd play beautiful music on the piano even if I never practiced again.

But I'd let my brother play his recorder even if it squawked. Maybe we'd even play duets.

If I were queen of the whole wide world, I'd make sure my brother never felt sad.

Sometimes I might even let him sit next
to my throne and pretend to be a king.

But NEVER
of the whole wide world.